ISBN: 9781793486165

Ars Omnia Press

Visit our website at:
www.sophiaomni.org

Sammy Snail's

A Little Time for . . . Quiet

Written and Illustrated by:
Marjorie S. Schiering

Sammy snail was very slow.
He glided over streets.
He talked about the daily sounds
with everyone he'd meet.

"It's true," he said, "I'm very sad.
I don't know what to say.
It seems the noise around me
is getting worse each day."

"The clatter and the clanging,
the sirens and the roar,
while even when we're sleeping
you can hear some people snore."

"Some noise must stop," he simply said.
"It's more than I can stand."
So, Sammy Snail went on his way
to ask for... a quiet land.

He went right up to Buddy Bullfrog
who lived just over there.
And, he asked him to be helpful and
please do his fair share.

"I see," said Buddy Bullfrog, "then
here's what we must do.
Go over to the train yard,
and down around the zoo."

"We'll tell everyone and everything
the best way they will hear
that we need a 'time for quiet'.
Let's, make it very clear."

"Going near and far and over there.
Tell everyone you see,
'this noise...it is not good for us.'
We'll be busy as the bees."

"Thank you," Sammy said to him.
"I'll go both near and far.
I'll travel over bridges, and
visit people in their cars."

"The days might be a little brighter,
the air a bit more clean.
I think everyone would smile,
and, I'd just simply beam!"

So, Sammy Snail went near and far
and softly said, "Please try it.
Let's have a part of every day
with a little time for quiet!"

Shhhhhhh.....

Dear Readers,

Dear Readers, the book you have just read is about how Sammy Snail is concerned with noise pollution. He asks everyone he meets to help reduce noise and then calls for every day having a little time for "quiet." This children's book is an introduction to "mindfulness."

What is that? Molloy College colleague, Mike Russo, refers to this being a time for paying attention to what you're thinking and feeling. It's a relaxing time, a time of being 'awake'. When a person pays attention to his/her relationship to things, they are seen most deeply. There may be creativity experienced, or critical thinking, or being/feeling fully aware of our surroundings... perhaps for later reference. In a way, when one is mindful they are being in-the-moment. So, Sammy Snail is suggesting we be mindful and take the time to be quiet during some part of each day. There's no better time to start mindfulness than as children or right now.

Made in the USA
Middletown, DE
06 January 2020